The Modern Ladies of Guanabacoa

by Eduardo Machado

No one shall make any changes in this title(s) for the purpose of production. No part of this book may be reproduced, stored in a retrieval system, scanned, uploaded, or transmitted in any form, by any means, now known or yet to be invented, including mechanical, electronic, digital, photocopying, recording, videotaping, or otherwise, without the prior written permission of the publisher. No one shall share this title(s), or any part of this title(s), through any social media or file hosting websites.

For all inquiries regarding motion picture, television, online/digital and other media rights, please contact Concord Theatricals Corp.

MUSIC AND THIRD-PARTY MATERIALS USE NOTE

Licensees are solely responsible for obtaining formal written permission from copyright owners to use copyrighted music and/or other copyrighted third-party materials (e.g., artworks, logos) in the performance of this play and are strongly cautioned to do so. If no such permission is obtained by the licensee, then the licensee must use only original music and materials that the licensee owns and controls. Licensees are solely responsible and liable for clearances of all third-party copyrighted materials, including without limitation music, and shall indemnify the copyright owners of the play(s) and their licensing agent, Concord Theatricals Corp., against any costs, expenses, losses and liabilities arising from the use of such copyrighted third-party materials by licensees. For music, please contact the appropriate music licensing authority in your territory for the rights to any incidental music.

IMPORTANT BILLING AND CREDIT REQUIREMENTS

If you have obtained performance rights to this title, please refer to your licensing agreement for important billing and credit requirements.

THE MODERN LADIES OF GUANABACOA was produced on January 26th, 1983 in New York City at the Ensemble Studio Theatre, with Curt Dempster as the artistic director. The prodcution was directed by James Hammerstein, with scenic and lighting design by Bennet Averyt, costume design by Deborah Shaw, sound design by Bruce Ellman, and original music composed by Rick Vartorella. The assistant scenic designer was Martha Gibson. the stage manager was Lisa Difranza, and the production stage manager was Teresa Elwert. The cast was as follows:

MARIA JOSEFA	Tresa Hughes
MANUELA	Ellen Barber
ARTURO	Larry Bryggman
ERNESTO	John Rothamn
MARIO	Stefano Loverso
MIGUEL	Robert Hallak
ADELITA	Julie Garfield
DOLORES GUTIERREZ	Susan Merson
OSCAR HERNANDES	Jose Santana

CHARACTERS

MARIA JOSEFA, *a Cuban woman, short, attractive, in her late forties*
ARTURO, *her husband, a Basque*
MANUELA, *their daughter, in her mid-twenties*
ERNESTO, *their eldest son*
MARIO, *their second son*
MIGUEL, *their youngest son*
DOLORES, *Maria Josefa's friend*
ADELITA, *Ernesto's wife, a very light mulatta*
OSCAR HERNANDEZ, *a taxi driver, thirty years old*

TIME

Act One: a spring day in 1928.
Act Two: a summer day in 1931.

PLACE

A middle-class home in Guanabacoa, Cuba.

*To the memory of my grandparents
Oscar Hernandez and Manuela Ripoll*

ACT ONE

Guanabacoa, Cuba, 1928. A middle-class home, Spanish in style, built at the end of the last century. The living room and dining room of the house are seen downstage center, with a door from the dining room leading to the offstage kitchen. The front door of the house, stage right, opens off the living room onto a small front porch, and there is a large back porch stage left. Both porches give access to the street. **MANUELA***'s bedroom is seen upstage center. A hallway leads to an offstage bathroom and to the other bedrooms of the house.*

MANUELA *is sitting in the living room, looking at a fashion magazine.* **MARIA JOSEFA** *enters. She is smoking a cigarette.*

MANUELA. Short hair! Short hair! Short hair! Mama, the answer to all my prayers.

MARIA JOSEFA. The neighbors still talk about my cigarettes. What would they say about short hair?

MANUELA. That it's wicked, that only women of ill repute do it.

MARIA JOSEFA. No short hair. No.

MANUELA. Nuns cut their hair!

MARIA JOSEFA. Nuns do it as a sacrifice to the Lord Jesus and the Virgin Mary. To show they're not vain about earthly things, not for style's sake. That's different.

MANUELA. Look, Mama, cool this summer. It'll be so convenient. Easy to take care of when I'm working.

MARIA JOSEFA. *(Glancing at magazine)* Beautiful, stylish; look how it looks when they curl it; your father would never allow it.

MANUELA. I'm twenty-seven years old. I should have a say.

MARIA JOSEFA. As long as you live under his roof and above his floor, you have to do what he likes. Always remember that. Memorize what I just told you. He feels bad enough about Ramon.

MANUELA. What about Ramon! I'm the one that should feel bad.

MARIA JOSEFA. Father only worries. Ramon and you were engaged for seven years, then you didn't get married, and he worries about that all the time.

MANUELA. It's not my fault, Mama. He died. *(She sobs)*

MARIA JOSEFA. Yes, but what man wants another man's bride.

MANUELA. I'm a good girl. I'll be a virgin on my wedding night.

MARIA JOSEFA. Did he kiss you? Manuela, did Ramon kiss you?

MANUELA. Mama! Don't embarrass me.

MARIA JOSEFA. Tell me, did Ramon kiss you before he died, Manuela?

MANUELA. Yes, Mama, he did.

MARIA JOSEFA. Your father's right. I'm a terrible chaperone. Men are haunted by things like that. Men want their women to only have kissed them; you should know that. Do not tell your father.

MANUELA. Oh, someone has a hex on me. It's not my fault. *(She prays silently and beats her breast three times)* Oscar has been saying hello to me.

MARIA JOSEFA. Oscar Hernandez?

MANUELA. Yes, the taxicab driver, Estrella's cousin?

MARIA JOSEFA. He works for Americans.

MANUELA. No.

MARIA JOSEFA. That's what people say, they're always saying that he drives Americans around all day long. That's what they say about him.

MANUELA. He drives a taxicab!

MARIA JOSEFA. Manuela, your father wants you to marry a man with a business. Just because your brother married trash...

MANUELA. I think she's nice.

MARIA JOSEFA. Ah, mulatta. *(She makes the sign of the cross)* Pray to God my grandson turns out light.

MANUELA. She's light. You can hardly tell.

MARIA JOSEFA. I can tell. Your father won't consent till he approves of your choice; but when he approves it'll be the right man.

MANUELA. Where's Papa, anyway? He's late for lunch.

MARIA JOSEFA. Eating with a business acquaintance – business.

MANUELA. Who?

MARIA JOSEFA. Let me see the magazine. *(Takes magazine)* Oh, what I like are the dresses and the pearls hanging so far down. Oh, especially the black mark by the lip. Exotic, but refined. The man who sells him eggs.

MANUELA. Please, Mama, let's cut it. We'll be the modern ladies of Guanabacoa.

MARIA JOSEFA. They already say I'm trying to be a Yankee because of the cigarettes. *(The clock strikes twelve.)*

MANUELA. What's wrong with that; they're the richest nation in the world.

MARIA JOSEFA. They're a bunch of gangsters. Manuela, lunch! Your brother will be here in a flash.

MANUELA. Who's eating?

MARIA JOSEFA. Just Mario; Miguel is eating out.

MANUELA. Or having affairs, no doubt.

MARIA JOSEFA. He's a young man; they have special needs. Young ladies shouldn't and don't understand the needs young men have.

(They exit into kitchen. We hear talking offstage. **MARIO** *and* **MIGUEL** *enter. They're whispering.)*

MARIO. How do you know it was him; maybe it was someone that looked like him.

MIGUEL. Who else in Cuba is that tall? Blond, blue eyes and speaks with a Basque accent.

MARIO. He shouldn't do things like that in town; what if someone else saw him?

MIGUEL. She seduced him; he couldn't say no; what do you expect, he's a man.

MARIO. But the gringo's wife; he should be careful. He overbought again too many eggs, five extra pigs. He's such a fool.

MIGUEL. You should feel proud; because Father is the greatest stud in the province of Havana.

MARIO. He fools around, we take care of the business, he overbuys to prove that he's running a successful store, then he goes out into the street and conquers while we work.

(**MANUELA** *and* **MARIA JOSEFA** *enter with food.*)

MIGUEL. What are we having today?

MARIA JOSEFA. Fried bananas, rice and baked fish. Don't worry, Miguel, there's plenty for you.

MANUELA. Did the young lady not serve hot lunch today?

MARIO. Manuela! That dress shows too much.

MANUELA. Too much of what?

MARIO. Your breast. People will talk. You have to be careful.

MANUELA. Oh. I'm sorry.

MARIA JOSEFA. Pay attention to your brothers. It's their reputation at stake.

MIGUEL. No one wants a trollop for a sister.

MARIO. Do not use that language! Have respect for your mother and sister, Miguel!

MARIA JOSEFA. Manuela wanted to cut her hair.

MARIO. You said no.

MIGUEL. Only Yankees cut their hair.

MANUELA. Let me serve you lunch, Mario.

MARIO. Thank you, sister.

MANUELA. How much fish?

MARIO. Just a little bit.

MARIA JOSEFA. Aren't you hungry?

MIGUEL. I am.

MARIO. That's enough.

MARIA JOSEFA. I'll serve you.

MIGUEL. Thank you, Mama.

MARIO. That's plenty. Where's Father?

MARIA JOSEFA. With a business acquaintance. Didn't he tell you?

MARIO. Oh, yes. The man who sells…

MANUELA. Eggs.

MIGUEL. Yes, eggs.

MARIA JOSEFA. No more talk.

> (*They eat, except* **MANUELA**, *who continues to serve, pouring water, etc.*)

MARIO. Mama, the fish doesn't have enough salt.

MIGUEL. I think it needs pepper.

MARIO. I can't eat it.

MARIA JOSEFA. I'll fry you two eggs; they go well with rice – and bananas.

MARIO. You don't have to, but if you want to, fine.

MARIA JOSEFA. Of course, my darling. I'm glad your father isn't here to taste it. And you, Miguel, do you like it? Can you eat it?

MIGUEL. I'm fine.

> (**MARIA JOSEFA** *exits to the kitchen.*)

Has anyone heard from Ernesto?

MANUELA. He's married now. (*She giggles*)

MARIO. That shouldn't matter; a child's first duty is to his parents. It's one of the commandments. No man can love any woman as much as his own mother, because no woman on earth suffered the way she did to give him life. Even Christ loved his mother more than mankind.

MIGUEL. Manuela, another piece of fish.

(She takes his plate, serves him.)

MANUELA. Is that enough?

MIGUEL. A little more. Thank you.

MANUELA. My pleasure.

MARIO. Manuela, always remember, a daughter's loyalty is first to her father. That's whose name you carry to your death.

MANUELA. In America, they get their husband's name.

MARIO. Americans! Manuela! No matter who you marry, first is your father, then your family, then your husband.

MANUELA. No one will ever take Papa's place.

(MARIA JOSEFA enters.)

MARIA JOSEFA. Two eggs, my darling. I sprinkled lots of salt. Here's some fresh rice. Do you want me to mix them for you?

MARIO. Yes, Mama, you're a saint.

(She mixes them and feeds MARIO.)

MARIA JOSEFA. My two handsome boys; now taste it. Is it good, Mario, yes?

MARIO. Hmmmmmm. *(He nods yes)*

MARIA JOSEFA. Manuela, Mario's dirty plates. Into the kitchen.

(MANUELA takes MARIO's dirty plates.)

MIGUEL. And bring back some more water.

MARIA JOSEFA. And start boiling water for cafe.

MANUELA. All right. *(She exits)*

MARIA JOSEFA. Do you really like it?

MARIO. Delicious.

MARIA JOSEFA. I have some sad and shocking news that I feel I must tell you. I talked to Dolores Gutirez. And now you two must do something about it.

(MARIO and MIGUEL look at each other in terror.)

MIGUEL. What?

MARIO. She's just a gossip.

MARIA JOSEFA. She saw Adelita dancing with another man.

MARIO. Where?

MIGUEL. Adelita?

MARIA JOSEFA. The mulatta.

> (**MANUELA** *enters.*)

MIGUEL. Ernesto's wife!

MARIO. God damn it, shit damn.

MANUELA. What's wrong?

> (*They eat.*)

> What about Ernesto's wife?

> (*They eat.*)

> What happened?

MARIA JOSEFA. Let's eat.

MARIO. Thank you, Mama. We'll take tare of her.

MANUELA. What did she do?

MIGUEL. She was seen tangoing with –

MARIA JOSEFA. Quiet.

MIGUEL. Never mind, sorry, Mama.

MARIO. Just don't spend a lot of time with her; be polite, you're her sister-in-law. She's pregnant with our brother's baby.

MARIA JOSEFA. Maybe!

MARIO. But don't trust her.

MANUELA. What has she done?

MARIA JOSEFA. She's making a cuckold out of your brother; she's putting horns on his head. (*She begins to cry*)

MANUELA. Oh God, poor Ernesto,

MIGUEL. She's been doing it in public, tangoing with a strange man.

MARIA JOSEFA. Enough talk, eat.
> (*Silence.*)

> The tango. Oh, help us, sweet blessed heart of Jesus Christ.

MARIO. Yes, Mama, you're right.

MIGUEL. Mama's always right, right?

MARIO. I'll set her straight. No brother of mine is going to be cuckolded.

MANUELA. We should tell him, he should know.

MARIO. Leave it to us.

MIGUEL. We know what to do.

MARIA JOSEFA. No more discussions.

> (**MANUELA** *finally starts to eat.*)

> Manuela, help me bring in the cafe.

> (**MANUELA** *and* **MARIA JOSEFA** *exit.*)

MARIO. Slut, she'd better confess.

MIGUEL. We'll get his name, and we'll beat the shit out of him. In the balls where it hurts.

MARIO. If she only danced with him we won't tell Ernesto. We'll just warn her and tell her it better not happen again. If there was more, we'll tell Ernesto and he can decide what to do.

MIGUEL. She's sneaky. How will we know she's telling the truth?

MARIO. We'll get his name from her, and the truth from him.

> (**MARIA JOSEFA** *carries a tray with four cups of cafe.* **MANUELA** *follows.*)

MARIA JOSEFA. Cafe, boys, cafe.

> (*They each take a cup and drink it in one gulp.*)

MARIO. Delicious.

MIGUEL. Now a nap.

MARIO. At work in a half-hour.

MANUELA. Don't worry, Mario. I'll wake him.

> (**MIGUEL** *exits.*)

MARIO. I have information to trace, Mama. Thank Dolores for us. Tell her to please keep it between us and her and make something nice for dinner.

(**MARIO** *exits,* **MANUELA** *eats,* **MARIA JOSEFA** *sips her café.*)

MARIA JOSEFA. Let's clear the dishes and the girl will do them later.

MANUELA. I'm so worried.

MARIA JOSEFA. Don't think about it; your brothers will take care of it.

(*They gather the dishes.*)

MANUELA. I think the fish tastes fine.

MARIA JOSEFA. Mario likes special attention, that's all. He's a little spoiled; I spoiled him; he'll find a good wife.

MANUELA. What would we do without him and Papa.

(*They clear the dishes onto a tray.*)

Mama, I have a confession...

MARIA JOSEFA. What is it, Manuela?

MANUELA. Well, you see…

MARIA JOSEFA. Tell me, Manuela!

MANUELA. Oscar is coming today, to ask permission. To call on me in the evenings.

MARIA JOSEFA. When did he ask you? Where did you speak to him, when?

MANUELA. At the dance for "Our Lady of the Immaculate Conception."

MARIA JOSEFA. Do you know him? Did Mario speak to him?

MANUELA. Yes, he did. He asked me to dance five times.

MARIA JOSEFA. Did he kiss you?!

MANUELA. No, Mama, he did not!

MARIA JOSEFA. He was polite?

MANUELA. Yes. He wants to call on me, he said he'd come by and ask permission. He's a gentleman, Mama, he's handsome.

MARIA JOSEFA. Hope your father likes him, let's hope he likes him.

MANUELA. Let's pray that he likes him. I like him.

MARIA JOSEFA. Be proper, remember, be proper.

MANUELA. I will, you raised me right. Can I try a cigarette?

MARIA JOSEFA. All right, but don't tell your father. He knows
1 smoke but never in front of him.

(*They smoke cigarettes.*)

You're right, Manuela, short hair is attractive. I bet it
looks great with cigarettes.

MANUELA. It does, Mama, look at this picture. (*She puts her
hair up and poses with a cigarette*)

MARIA JOSEFA. We'll mention it to your father. He likes his
two ladies to be up-to-date.

MANUELA. It's truly European.

MARIA JOSEFA. That won't help with Arturo the Basque.

(**MANUELA** *winds the Victrola. It plays. They smoke and
look at the magazine.* **ARTURO** *enters.*)

ARTURO. Put out the cigarettes, I want lunch in ten minutes, I'm hungry.

MARIA JOSEFA. I thought they took you out to lunch.

ARTURO. He only bought me drinks.

MANUELA. I'll make you a banana omelet.

MARIA JOSEFA. And warm up the rice.

ARTURO. Thank you, my sweet girl.

(**ARTURO** *blows* **MANUELA** *a kiss. She catches it, then
exits to the kitchen with tray of dishes.*)

Now I need a clean shirt.

MARIA JOSEFA. It's not hot today. I have things to talk to
you about. Oscar Hernandez wants to call on Manuela.
What do you think?

ARTURO. Did you give him permission?

MARIA JOSEFA. He's coming today to ask you for permission.

ARTURO. Fine, dear.

MARIA JOSEFA. We were thinking of cutting our hair in a
bob like they're doing now; it's the latest style, and 1

want to be in style so you never get bored. So you never want anything else, so you never go looking anywhere else, so you don't have a roving eye. Adelita was seen tangoing with a man. Mario's looking into it. What is Ernesto going to do? I wonder if it's his baby?

ARTURO. Just gossip, don't listen to gossips.

MARIA JOSEFA. But you have to check things out. I don't want my son to be a cuckold. I want our family to be respected. I never danced with anyone but you, not for thirty-four years. I was fourteen. You're the handsomest man, they all look like cockroaches next to you. I love you. I adore you, only you. *(She is standing next to him)* You smell like perfume.

ARTURO. Manuela! Is lunch ready.

MANUELA. Not yet, Papa.

MARIA JOSEFA. You do, you smell like perfume.

ARTURO. It's the combination of my cologne and sweat. That's why I need a fresh shirt.

MARIA JOSEFA. I'll help Manuela. Hurry up.

(**ARTURO** *exits to the bathroom and* **MARIA JOSEFA** *to the kitchen. There is a knock at the door.*

MANUELA *enters, opens the door.)*

MANUELA. Oscar. Let me call my mother.

OSCAR. Yes, of course. I'll wait outside.

MANUELA. Mama. Mama, come here for a moment.

(**MARIA JOSEFA** *enters.)*

MARIA JOSEFA. What is it? *(She goes to the door)* Oh, Oscar, please come in.

OSCAR. People talk in this town, but they don't talk about you and they never will. You are so proper.

MARIA JOSEFA. Thank you.

MANUELA. Thank you.

OSCAR. Columbus said Cuban women are the most beautiful and chaste. You are the image he was talking about.

MANUELA. Thank you, Oscar.

MARIA JOSEFA. Yes. Would you like to sit down? Cafe? A cold glass of water? Anything.

OSCAR. Thank you. But I have to get back to work. I came to ask for permission, if I may come tonight and call on Manuela. If I may?

MARIA JOSEFA. Well, it's up to her father.

OSCAR. To the butcher shop, thank you.

MANUELA. No, he's here! I'll get him.

OSCAR. Don't wake him!

MANUELA. He's not taking a nap. *(She exits)*

MARIA JOSEFA. Can I get you some dessert, lemonade, crackers?

OSCAR. No thank you, I'm fine.

MARIA JOSEFA. Do you mind if I smoke?

OSCAR. Not at all, I think it's attractive.

MARIA JOSEFA. It's one of my few vanities.

MANUELA. He'll be here in a minute.

ARTURO *(Offstage)* Wake up, my lazy son, wake up.

MIGUEL *(Offstage)* Shit! Oh sorry, Papa.

ARTURO *(Offstage)* Get to work. *(He enters)* Yes.

OSCAR. Well, sir, I would like to call on your daughter tonight.

ARTURO. Fine. Be here at eight-thirty; be out of here at ten.

OSCAR. Thank you, sir.

(**MIGUEL** *enters,* **MARIA JOSEFA** *exits to the kitchen.*)

MIGUEL. You didn't wake me, Manuela, I'm late.

MANUELA. You said half an hour.

MIGUEL. I have to get to work. *(He exits)*

OSCAR. Till eight-thirty, sir. Till eight-thirty, Manuela.

MANUELA. Yes, Oscar.

OSCAR. *(Exiting)* I'll drive you, Miguel.

ARTURO. Lunch, Manuela.

MANUELA. Yes, Papa. Thank you.

MARIA JOSEFA. Here is your lunch.

(**ARTURO** *eats.*)

MANUELA. Anything else?

ARTURO. Just for you to sit by me. You'll be my girl forever, won't you.

MANUELA. Yes, Papa, forever.

ARTURO. I hear you want to cut your hair.

MANUELA. Yes.

MARIA JOSEFA. I don't know...

MANUELA. It's in style, styles change.

(**MARIA JOSEFA** *looks through the magazine.*)

MARIA JOSEFA. Maybe she's right, but is it feminine?

MANUELA. I think so, please, Papa.

ARTURO. Maybe, we'll talk about it later.

MANUELA. Please, Papa!

ARTURO. But I like my sweet girl's long hair.

DOLORES (*On the porch*) It's me, Maria, have a glass of water for an old friend?

ARTURO. Dolores the gossip, your source of information.

MARIA JOSEFA. Be quiet. Don't embarrass me, please. Arturo, you know about her husband and the night-club singer in Havana. Please be polite. Please. (*She goes to answer the door*)

DOLORES. Maria.

(*They kiss.*)

My sweet poor dear friend.

(**ARTURO** *exits to the kitchen.*)

MARIA JOSEFA. Good news, Manuela has an appointment tonight. Oscar Hernandez the taxicab driver, Estrella's cousin. What do you think?

DOLORES. Does he know about Ramon?

MARIA JOSEFA. He must. He was at the funeral.

DOLORES. That's right. Ramon and he went to school together; he's very handsome, a little... you know. *(She indicates by touching her skin that he is dark)*

MARIA JOSEFA. No, he's light, you can hardly tell. It was his great-great-grandmother's mother.

*(**ARTURO** enters with a glass of water on a plate, and gives it to **DOLORES**.)*

ARTURO. The Moors conquered you Spaniards for five hundred years.

DOLORES. Arturo, having lunch. It's so late.

ARTURO. A businessman's life is hurried nowadays.

DOLORES. Yes, the business.

ARTURO. Running a business is hard work.

*(**ARTURO** cuts one bite of his omelet. **DOLORES** looks at him.)*

Well. I'm done. I'm going.

MANUELA. No cafe? You hardly ate. Was the omelet over-done?

ARTURO. Later, sweetheart.

DOLORES. Walk your father to work, keep him company.

ARTURO. Why?

DOLORES. You'll miss her when she's married and not yours anymore.

MANUELA. It'd be nice to take a walk.

ARTURO. Come then. I like having pretty girls walking me down the street.

DOLORES. You do, don't you?

ARTURO. Goodbye, Dolores, see you again. Goodbye, sweet-ness, I'm working late.

MARIA JOSEFA. Be sure to come in time to see Oscar, please. He'll be here at eight-thirty.

ARTURO. I'll be home at ten.

MARIA JOSEFA. Goodbye, dear.

*(**ARTURO** and **MANUELA** exit.)*

I'll get us cafe.

DOLORES. Sit down, Maria, take a deep breath, 1 have some sad news.

MARIA JOSEFA. What? It's not Ernesto's baby?

DOLORES. I just have to say it fast because it breaks my heart. I saw Arturo with Beatrice the American. They went into a hotel. They used the room for two hours. I'm sorry I had to tell you, but I am your friend.

MARIA JOSEFA. It was him and her?

DOLORES. Yes.

MARIA JOSEFA. Thank you, Dolores. My family is dishonored. *(She finishes* **DOLORES***'s water)* Cafe?

DOLORES. No. Do you need anything?

MARIA JOSEFA. No, thank you. *(She gets a cigarette and lets her hair down. She looks at herself in the mirror)* There's no portrait of me, no record of my youth except what people remember. I dreamed Arturo caressed me, I caressed him back. It was as simple as that. My compulsions. My sorrow gets in the way.

DOLORES. Should I stay with you for a moment?

MARIA JOSEFA. Yes. It's my fault, I've tried to be good.

DOLORES. You are good.

MARIA JOSEFA. Can I tell you a secret? Between us? Between just these walls?

DOLORES. Of course, we've been friends all our lives.

MARIA JOSEFA. I was so afraid not to follow the rules that I never found the essence.

DOLORES. The essence – there's no essence. That's the table, it's there; the sun is warm, you feel it, you have a home, you get fed. It's real. It's life.

MARIA JOSEFA. And afterwards, there's heaven?

DOLORES. Of course.

MARIA JOSEFA. And we'll levitate.

DOLORES. We'll float up to Christ.

MARIA JOSEFA. And he'll caress our faces and stroke our hair, feel our pulse and cover us with kisses.

DOLORES. He blows into your mouth to bring you back to life, but that's when he comes back, and we get our bodies back. After death just your spirit floats up.

MARIA JOSEFA. And we float because we followed his rules.

DOLORES. Yes.

MARIA JOSEFA. It's worth the wait,

DOLORES. Yes, dear.

MARIA JOSEFA. Yes it is.

(They kiss. **MARIA JOSEFA** *goes to the mirror and looks at her hair. She touches it.)*

A caress, that's what life is. It's pretty. It's still pretty.

(Blackout. Lights up, **MARIA JOSEFA, MANUELA, MARIO, MIGUEL** *and* **ERNESTO** *are sitting at the table eating custard.* **MARIA JOSEFA** *is sitting next to* **ERNESTO.***)*

MIGUEL. This guy walks up to another guy. He says, "How much do you weigh?" The other guy answers, "A hundred and sixty-five pounds exactly." The other guy shoots him. Bang. Bang. The guy who shot tells the other guy, "A hundred and sixty-five pounds and two ounces."

(No one laughs.)

The bullet weighed two ounces. BANG! BANG!

(Some of them laugh.)

ERNESTO. Where's Papa?

MARIO. Working.

ERNESTO. Oh, I see, poor Papa.

MARIA JOSEFA. Manuela, eat something.

MANUELA. I'm nervous!

MIGUEL. Because of her beau.

ERNESTO. Oscar! Oscar! Oscar!

MARIO. Where's your wife?

MARIA JOSEFA. Not now.

ERNESTO. At her mother's. I have a free night. *(He laughs)*

MARIO. At her mother's. Oh, you left her there?

ERNESTO. Of course. Two farmers go to a big theatre in Havana. They get seats far away from each other. One farmer says to the other farmer, "As soon as the show is over, find me so we don't miss the bus." They sit. The show is over. The one farmer gets up and yells, "Jose, we're going to miss the bus." A lady goes up to him and says, "Sir, this is a respectable theatre, please don't yell." The farmer says, "I have to find Jose." The lady says, "Here, use my binoculars." He finds Jose. He looks like he's standing right there. He whispers, "Jose, we're going to miss the bus."

(They laugh.)

MARIO. You're picking her up?

ERNESTO. Of course, more custard.

MIGUEL. Oh, Oscar, my love.

MANUELA. Stop it.

MARIA JOSEFA. Stop it, Miguel!

*(***MIGUEL*** starts to sing.)*

Too bad for your father, he's missing all the fun but it must be worth it.

MARIO. What?

MARIA JOSEFA. His business.

MARIO. Of course, it keeps us alive.

ERNESTO, MARIO & MIGUEL. *(Singing)*
Days dancing free and in love.
Hours full of passion and song.
The days and the hours that we wait.
For that one look full of passion and song.
Days filled with endless desire.

Hours when desire turns to pain.
The pain of the hours that we wait.
For that one look
full of passion and song.

MANUELA. Stop it Ernesto, Miguel.

ERNESTO. My favorite, most beautiful lady, your married son still has to come home for a good dinner.

MARIA JOSEFA. Do you think I'm beautiful?

ERNESTO. Like an Italian painting.

MIGUEL. It's hard to find a woman that compares with you.

ERNESTO. When I went to school, no mother was ever like you.

MARIA JOSEFA. Oh, I've gotten old. But I do have handsome sons who'll take care of me, yes?

ERNESTO. Yes, Mama.

MIGUEL. Till we hit our graves.

MARIA JOSEFA. Hold my hand, Miguel. Hold my hand, Ernesto. And keep me company, before anyone else, before wives and children and girlfriends.

ERNESTO. Always, Mama. Always. *(He kisses her on the forehead)*

MIGUEL. Yours, Mama.

MARIA JOSEFA. Let's clear the table.

(The women clear as the men light cigars and smoke.)

MARIO. Two guys are at a bullring. Across the way one of the guys sees a beautiful girl. He tells his friend, "Look, I'm going to marry that girl." His friend asks, "Which one?" The guy points at her again. "That one over on the other side." The friend asks, "Which one?" The guy takes out his gun. Bang. Bang.

*(**OSCAR** knocks on the front door, **MARIO** goes to answer it.)*

Oscar.

OSCAR. Mario.

MARIO. Pleasure to see you.

ERNESTO. Oscar.

OSCAR. Ernesto.

MIGUEL. Oscar, thanks for the ride.

MARIO. I'll get Mama.

MIGUEL. Ernesto, I'll be out on the porch.

ERNESTO. Dominos?

MIGUEL. Of course. *(He exits to porch)*

OSCAR. How's married life?

ERNESTO. Oh all right, you know women.

OSCAR. Yes.

(**MARIA JOSEFA** *enters.*)

ERNESTO. See you later on.

OSCAR. Good evening, Maria, how are you tonight.

(**ERNESTO** *exits to porch and plays dominos with* **MIGUEL.**)

MARIA JOSEFA. Fine. Fine. Manuela.

MANUELA *(Offstage)* Yes.

MARIA JOSEFA. Oscar is here.

(**MANUELA** *enters.*)

OSCAR. Good evening. Wonderful to see you.

MANUELA. The same.

(**MARIO** *walks through on his way to the porch.*)

MARIA JOSEFA. Mario, sit with them while I get the cafe.

OSCAR. Ah, cafe. Thank you.

MARIO. Come and sit,

(**OSCAR** *waits for* **MANUELA** *to sit first, then* **MARIO** *sits, then* **OSCAR.** *They all stare at each other smiling for about two minutes. Once in a while* **MANUELA** *and* **OSCAR** *look at each other for a second.*)

OSCAR. What a comfortable sofa.

MANUELA. Yes.

OSCAR. Ah, the smell of cafe.

(**MARIA JOSEFA** *enters with cups of cafe on a tray.*)

MARIA JOSEFA. Excuse me, Oscar, I'll serve the boys first, then we can sit and talk.

OSCAR. No trouble.

MARIO. Are you sure?

OSCAR. I'm positive.

(MARIA JOSEFA *goes to the porch.*)

MARIO. What would we do without cafe.

OSCAR. Yes, cafe. It used to be a religious drink.

MANUELA. Really.

(MARIA JOSEFA *enters.*)

MARIA JOSEFA. Oscar?

OSCAR. Thank you. *(He smells his cafe)* The aroma.

MARIA JOSEFA. Mario. *(Gives him cafe)*

MARIO. Thank you.

OSCAR. It was discovered under –

MARIO. I'm going outside for a while.

OSCAR. – very interesting circumstances.

MARIA JOSEFA. And one for Manuela.

MANUELA. And one for you.

(MARIA JOSEFA *sits.*)

OSCAR. It's still like a religious service.

MARIA JOSEFA. What is.

MANUELA. Cafe, Oscar was talking about cafe.

MARIA JOSEFA. Oh. Cafe. Yes?

OSCAR. The name derives from the Arabic "Kahwah."

MANUELA. Kahwah?

OSCAR. Kahwah makes an aromatic beverage which is very valued which is made into brew with toasted and ground coffee seeds. In the thirteenth century a preaching Arabian mulatto observed how the cows after they ate the fruits of some trees became animated. He noticed a certain activity which departed from the norm and that it was a direct result from the trees and leaves they were eating. Well, the Arab, after noticing, prepared, with the grain of the before-mentioned kahwah, a brew which became a part of his religious ceremonies. The results were stupendous. His followers were able to stay awake through all the religious services.

MANUELA. How interesting, Oscar.

OSCAR. Since then, the use of coffee became generalized in Egypt's Pergia. It was introduced in Europe in 1660, passing through the French Antilles and later to South America.

MARIA JOSEFA. You must read a great deal. Mario, come in here. It's very interesting. Miguel, Ernesto, you too.

(They come in and stand by the door.)

MANUELA. I'm sorry, Oscar, we must be embarrassing you.

OSCAR. Not at all, dear. Anyway…

MANUELA. *(To herself)* Dear. *(She smiles)*

OSCAR. As the years passed, coffee began to become a habit according to the different customs of each different country. In each country, it had a special characteristic. In some countries, a small cup of coffee is used to welcome visitors.

MANUELA. Like here in Cuba.

OSCAR. It's become more frequent an expression these days. To offer a small cup of aromatic cafe is to bring a note of courtesy to a reunion.

MARIA JOSEFA. Beautifully said, almost poetic, Oscar. *(She signals the boys to sit)*

OSCAR. In Europe as well as America, coffee shops became famous, where scholars and students seated around a table with their respective cups of aromatic cafe discussed very passionately, politics, literature, poetics and art. Some of these establishments, like…Merchants' Coffee House, have become a part of history.

MANUELA. Really?

OSCAR. It was there in 1717, no 1774, a "Committee of Correspondence" started by New Yorkian patriots, sent a letter to a group of Bostonians proposing the union of American colonies.

MARIO. Very interesting.

ERNESTO. And they drink such weak coffee.

MARIO. Like dirty water.

MIGUEL. I could never drink it.

MANUELA. Shh.

MARIA JOSEFA. Continue.

OSCAR. Well, today the producers of the fabulous bean are Colombia, Brazil –

MANUELA. Not just us?

OSCAR. – Guatemala, El Salvador, Mexico, Costa Rica, Hondutas, Haiti, Santo Domingo, Puerto Rico, Cuba.

MARIO. For the best!

OSCAR. True, but it's even cultivated in Ethiopia.

MANUELA. Ethiopia, Africa!

OSCAR. Yes, today in the entire world, one always savors a small cup of the brown nectar from the white gods.

(They applaud.)

MARIA JOSEFA. So well put, I'm making another round. Bring in the cups.

MARIO. I'll get mine.

ERNESTO. *(Simultaneously)* Make mine with milk, Mama.

(The three go into the kitchen, **MIGUEL** *stays and chaperones.* **MANUELA** *looks at him.)*

MIGUEL. Me too. *(He exits to the kitchen)*

*(***OSCAR** *gives* **MANUELA** *a note.)*

OSCAR. I adore you.

(They kiss.)

MANUELA. My love.

MARIA JOSEFA. *(Offstage):* In the kitchen, children.

MANUELA. On our way, Mama.

(They go into the kitchen. **ARTURO** *enters; he goes to bedrooms. We hear running water.* **MARIA JOSEFA** *enters. In the kitchen,* **MIGUEL** *is telling jokes we heard earlier.)*

MARIA JOSEFA. Taking a shower so late at night?

(*The water stops.* **ARTURO** *comes into the living room.*)

Your sons are here. Where were you?

ARTURO. Working, darling, my sweetheart, working.

MARIA JOSEFA. They're in the kitchen. Say hello to Oscar.

(**ARTURO** *goes into the kitchen.* **MARIA JOSEFA** *sits on the front porch in a place where the rest won't see her when they enter. She lights a cigarette, leaves the front door open.*)

ARTURO. (*Offstage*) Miguel, Mario, Ernesto, say hello to your father. Oscar, good evening. Manuela, let the men talk for a while.

(**MANUELA** *enters and goes into her bedroom.*)

MANUELA. Oscar, Oscar, Oscar Hernandez. The lips feel nice. (*She gets lipstick, rubs it on*) Oh what a thought. I won't have to wait anymore. Oh what a thought. Oscar Hernandez.

(*The men enter the living room.*)

ERNESTO. The store was quiet, we did not sell enough again today. We are not making enough money.

ARTURO. It'll get better.

ERNESTO. I don't know, Papa, you are buying too much; today we received twenty dozen eggs from Paco, when you know we only sell ten.

ARTURO. I owe Paco a favor, he is my friend, what's an extra couple of dozens.

MARIO. If you keep overbuying we will not make it this month. I still haven't taken my salary for last week. You owe me a week!

ARTURO. You two have to learn, men help each other that's how the world got this far. Have pride. What's a couple of dozen eggs? Pride, that's life.

MARIO. We are ordering too much.

ARTURO. We'll discuss this at work not at home, goodnight. (*To* **OSCAR**) Ten o'clock. (*He exits*)

OSCAR. Goodnight, sir. Ernesto, the problem is not over-buying, it's knowing what to sell.

MARIO. What to sell, that's right; Ernesto, Oscar's right.

ERNESTO. We sell meat.

MANUELA. Enough business for one night.

OSCAR. It's important, Manuela, it is the future; I'll see you tomorrow at eight-thirty.

MANUELA. At eight.

OSCAR. Then at eight, whatever you say.

MANUELA. Goodnight.

OSCAR. Sleep well.

(She exits.)

MARIO. Don't say goodnight to your brothers.

(She comes back and kisses her brothers on the forehead. She exits.)

OSCAR. The business for the decade of the thirties is transportation. Transportation.

ERNESTO. Transportation?

MARIO. Taxis?

OSCAR. No, bigger than that; buses, you can carry thirty passengers, five cents a ride.

ERNESTO. Highways, yes.

OSCAR. To Havana and back. Five of us have talked to the transportation authority, and they're going to give us the routes in the province of Havana. All I need is capital and they'll give me my own routes. That's my plan.

MARIO. Let's go to a bar. Oscar? Ernesto?

ERNESTO. Yes, let's do that.

OSCAR. I have my taxi, ready to go?

ERNESTO. Five cents a ride?

MARIO. Miguel!

MIGUEL. Yes?

MARIO. To a bar.

MIGUEL. All right.

OSCAR. The automobile, no more trains or boats or horses. Transportation, that's the money in the future.

(They exit. **MARIA JOSEFA** *enters the living room.)*

MARIA JOSEFA. The future, the thirties. Youth, hope, ambition. Hope, no remorse, without lies. Who defeats my fiercest foes? Who revives my fainting heart? Who is life in life to me? What's the high reward I win? Whose name do I glory in?

(ARTURO *enters in his robe.)*

ARTURO. To bed, dear.

MARIA JOSEFA. Not now, not ever. I won't ever touch you. I won't ever touch a man. I won't ever look at you. I'm tired of being confused. I'm tired of being tormented.

ARTURO. What are you talking about?

MARIA JOSEFA. A hotel room at lunch before dinner; sneaking off with Americans. Adultery; being made a fool!

ARTURO. You shouldn't listen to gossips.

MARIA JOSEFA. Because gossips tell the truth. Because gossips see and report it. Because gossips see you deceiving me. I never had another man touch me. I've always stayed at home. I get up early and make the cafe, boil the milk, wash the clothes, keep everyone clean, prepare the lemonade. I do the job.

ARTURO. And I've always been discreet. I'll always keep it out of your eyes, out of the house, that's what men are supposed to do. Let's go to sleep.

MARIA JOSEFA. No I have something to do. I'm getting rid of this. (*She touches her hair*)

ARTURO. I give my permission. Goodnight. *(He exits)*

MARIA JOSEFA. I did the job twelve times. Arturo de la Asuncion Ripoll born July 16, 1895. Died at birth. Ernesto born June 7, 1898. Manuela born January I, 1901, she grew up to be his true love. Mario born December 22, 1906. Fernando de la Asuncion Ripoll born July 23, 1907, died October 30, 1907- Gilda de la Asuncion

Ripoll born May 29, 1909, died June 10, 1909, Miguel born March 10, 1911, Pepe de la Asuncion Ripoll born March 7, 1912, died four months later, Antonia de la Asuncion Ripoll born April 22, 1913, died December 23, 1913, all the babies that went from the womb to the breast to the grave. I had no milk, so they died. Olga de la Asuncion Ripoll born November 18, 1915, born dead, and the one that was early and died the next day, Eurgenio de la Asuncion Ripoll. Enrique born November 14, 1902. Died aged eleven, December 26, 1913. There was something wrong with his blood. That is my life with him and he talks about discretion. *(She gets scissors)* Manuela dear, wake up. Father gave us his permission. We're cutting our hair. We are going to be in style, dear.

(Blackout.)

END OF ACT ONE

ACT TWO

Three years later. 1931. The set is the same but all the furnishings, which are Art Deco in style, are new. **ARTURO**, **MARIA JOSEFA**, **MANUELA**, **ADELITA** *and* **DOLORES** *are in the living room. The women all have short hair and are dressed like flappers.* **MANUELA** *is nine months pregnant. The song "Sheik of Araby," sung by Rudi Vallee, is playing on the Victrola.*

ARTURO. What is he saying?

ADELITA. It's a tribute to Valentino. They idolized him in the USA; they like exotic people.

MARIA JOSEFA. Tell me, Adelita, is it the custom in America... to leave the only grandson at the mother's mother's house?

ADELITA. He fell asleep, 1 didn't want to wake him.

DOLORES. Discover Cuba first, and North America later.

ADELITA. Delicious meal, Maria.

MANUELA. I cooked it, Adelita.

DOLORES. Good for you, Manuela, this family is full of hard-working people.

ARTURO. Did Oscar tell you when he was coming back, Manuela?

MANUELA. No, Papa.

ARTURO. Adelita, did Ernesto tell you when they were coming back?

MARIA JOSEFA. They should be here soon, Ernesto told me it was an important meeting.

DOLORES. Arturo, you must miss the butcher shop.

ARTURO. No, Dolores, I count the money at night. It's my job to guard the equipment. I protect the buses at night.

DOLORES. They shot two people in Havana last night.

MARIA JOSEFA. You know politicians, they don't even believe in Baby Jesus.

DOLORES. Oh Manuelita, you're so big, Manuelita pregnant.

ARTURO. Don't talk about it in front of me, I feel like hitting Oscar in the face.

(Sound of buses pulling up. Horns honk.)

MANUELA. Papa!

DOLORES. She's married now.

MARIA JOSEFA. She's expecting exactly nine months after the wedding night.

ADELITA. Just like me.

(We hear the men humming "We're in the Money": La La La La Money/ La La La La Money/ La La La La La La, La La La La Money. The men enter.)

ERNESTO. He did it! The transportation cooperative approved the request.

OSCAR. We have our dream.

ADELITA. I want to go for a ride.

MARIO. Not bad, Papa, we did it, two more buses.

MIGUEL. You want to see them?

ARTURO. No, everybody inside the house.

ERNESTO. He'll want another meeting.

ADELITA. Please, I want to go for a ride.

ERNESTO. Later, Adelita, not now. Papa wants us inside the house.

DOLORES. Two more buses, this family is on its way, will you remember your neighbors?

OSCAR. Always, Dolores. What kind of people do you think we are?

ARTURO. I need to talk to the men, time for business, you ladies go somewhere and talk.

DOLORES. I'll go to my house and leave the family alone, so you can celebrate.

MARIA JOSEFA. No, stay.

DOLORES. I'll talk to you tomorrow, goodnight. Congratulations, Oscar.

OSCAR. Thank you.

(DOLORES exits.)

MANUELA. I have to take a nap. I get tired all the time, nine months.

OSCAR. Are you happy?

MANUELA. Yes, Oscar. I'm glad about the buses. I'll ride one of them after the baby's born. *(She exits to the bedroom)*

MARIA JOSEFA. I'll be in the kitchen, there's dessert. Call me when you want it.

ERNESTO. What kind?

MARIA JOSEFA. Rum cake. *(She clears the table)*

ADELITA. Let me help you, Maria. *(She starts to help her)*

MARIA JOSEFA. That's all right, Adelita, I can do it. I'll take care of the dishes.

(She exits)

ADELITA. Yes, of course. I'm sorry.

(ADELITA goes. It is quiet for a moment.)

OSCAR. All the routes from Guanabacoa to Havana and the ones to Cojimar and they promised later on another bus and the routes to Regla.

ARTURO. I know the government is going to want a cut.

OSCAR. The government has been taken care of.

ARTURO. You talked to them?

OSCAR. Not directly.

ARTURO. You, Ernesto?

ERNESTO. No.

ARTURO. I like the way you take care of my money!

MARIO. Your money is in good hands; we are doing what we promised.

ARTURO. Who talked to them?

OSCAR. The cooperative, and they assured me that the government will not interfere. Arturo, all those pale, white Americans are saving any money they earn, to throw it all away for two weeks in the sun and the beach.

ARTURO. In the USA the market crashed.

OSCAR. Father, brothers, this is the most beautiful land that human eyes have seen. It was true when Christopher Columbus said it and it's true today. And Americans will spend anything they have for fun and the sun and we have that here in Cuba.

MIGUEL. We have the only safe business, Papa.

*(**MARIA JOSEFA** enters.)*

MARIA JOSEFA. Are you done? Is all the business taken care of? Who wants cake? You, Arturo?

ARTURO. No, I'll be leaving soon. It's my night to guard the equipment. They're not putting me out to pasture, I still have to work.

MIGUEL. You're still the bull, Papa.

ERNESTO. Mama, I want a great big piece of cake.

MARIA JOSEFA. My darling. I'll bring you a great big piece.

ERNESTO. I'll go with you. I'll taste it in the kitchen, then eat it in the living room.

*(**ERNESTO** and **MARIA JOSEFA** exit to the kitchen.)*

ARTURO. Your Yankee ideals will never work.

OSCAR. Free enterprise is knowing how to follow the plan. I know how.

ARTURO. Capitalism is falling apart. That's what a depression is.

OSCAR. We're not. You find what people want, need; be ready to get it; you charge them; they'll always pay it. Then you succeed anywhere at any time.

ARTURO. My father was a sheepherder. He never changed. My town stayed the same through the last war, Napoleon, the Moors. We live high up in the mountains and though Spain claims us as theirs, their territory, we know we're not. We know we're a tribe unto ourselves. We believe in no one. We know who we are.

OSCAR. Were you poor?

ARTURO. We ate.

OSCAR. Eating isn't enough anymore. We need different things. They've invented the automobile, a washing machine, a light bulb; and it's not what you eat anymore, it's how you cook it. Not just food, what kind of plates you eat it on –

(We hear **ADELITA** *singing.)*

– what forks you are using, on what kind of table – pine or mahogany. And we have to buy it. That's all.

ARTURO. I never had a thought like that. Never.

OSCAR. That's all right, I have.

ARTURO. Oscar? Rum? Brandy?

OSCAR. No, thank you.

> (**ARTURO, MIGUEL** *and* **MARIO** *drink their brandy;* **OSCAR** *goes out to the front porch;* **ADELITA** *is sitting there singing.)*
>
> Adelita.

ADELITA. *(Sings)* May I look for the one who is pure, may I keep all the things that endure…

OSCAR. I saw you.

ADELITA. So.

OSCAR. So? That's all you have to say, so.

ADELITA. No. So what!

OSCAR. What!

ADELITA. It means so what that you saw me. I saw you, too– What were you doing there?

OSCAR. Having a few drinks.

ADELITA. So was I.

OSCAR. What if somebody else saw you?

ADELITA. Then they saw me, so what.

OSCAR. Do you know what people say about you? What they

think about Ernesto? What people in the cooperative say about him?

ADELITA. I don't care to know.

OSCAR. If people keep on talking about you I'll have to get rid of Ernesto. This bus company is going to be a success —

ADELITA. We have two new buses, Oscar. We're doing very well.

OSCAR. We could have had the route to Regla, but people believe that my right hand and his wife should —

ADELITA. When they see you whoring in El Canon, no one cares. No one repeats it.

OSCAR. You won't repeat it?

ADELITA. No, Oscar.

OSCAR. Neither will I. But don't go back. It's bad for the business, for our reputation.

ADELITA. Don't worry, if I see you coming, I'll hide.

(**OSCAR** *goes back into the living room, he signals* **MARIO**, *we can hear* **ADELITA** *singing.*)

OSCAR. She's impossible.

MARIO. Yes.

OSCAR. We have to take care of it.

MARIO. Yes.

(**OSCAR** *exits into the bedroom.*)

ARTURO. What were you discussing.

MARIO. Nothing.

ARTURO. I want a report of everything that goes on, with our company.

MARIO. It's Ernesto.

ARTURO. What about him.

MARIO. He cannot handle the job.

ARTURO. That's not true, he's a good worker.

MARIO. The other partners in the cooperative won't deal with him. They do all the business with Oscar, Oscar makes all the arrangements about financing, the routes we'll get, everything. They won't deal with Ernesto.

ARTURO. Why won't they?

MARIO. They say he's too shy.

MIGUEL. He has no balls, Papa! I hate to say it, he's my brother but he has no real balls!

ARTURO. Shut up, Miguel! *(He hits* **MIGUEL***)*

MARIO. Miguel's right, anybody who stays at home while his wife goes to bars with other guys. What man could respect a man like that. And they don't want business dealings with him, they don't trust him.

ARTURO. They're going to have to. I'll deal with Ernesto.

*(***MARIO** *and* **MIGUEL** *start to exit to their rooms.)*

Where are you going?

MARIO. To get dressed, Papa. Get ready for the town.

MIGUEL. Some excitement, Papa!

ARTURO. That's right, show them, show them for your father.

MARIO. You're a legend, Papa.

ARTURO. That's true, I am. It comes from running around in the mountains fighting Spaniards. It gives you courage –

*(***MARIO** *and* **MIGUEL** *exit.* **ARTURO** *pours himself another drink. In the bedroom,* **MANUELA** *is asleep,* **OSCAR** *is getting dressed.* **MANUELA** *wakes up.)*

MANUELA. Oscar, come here. Oscar, don't leave. Oscar, sit next to me. My grandmother was just in this room with my little brother, Enrique. She told me she wanted me and my baby, that I had been chosen to go with them.

OSCAR. Oh, sweetie, a nightmare.

MANUELA. I said, "Oh, please, not my baby, not me. I can't go now. I'm too happy."

OSCAR. I'm glad she didn't take you.

MANUELA. She gestured "Fine," and walked away. My little brother said, "But we need a family member.

Remember?" Then they walked away. Don't go out. Stay with me. Hold me, caress me, Oscar.

OSCAR. You're pregnant.

MANUELA. It doesn't matter.

OSCAR. You'd get hurt. I couldn't take a chance then hurt you. What if the baby felt it, and it was born perverted? I couldn't take that risk. We shouldn't take the risk.

MANUELA. I need you.

OSCAR. I'm here.

MANUELA. I need you close. I'm shaking.

OSCAR. It was a nightmare.

MANUELA. No!

OSCAR. It's getting late.

MANUELA. Don't go away.

OSCAR. I have to.

MANUELA. Don't.

OSCAR. I'm late. Don't worry. The baby won't die.

MANUELA. Someone will.

OSCAR. I have to get dressed.

MANUELA. Let me watch while you get dressed. I like looking at your feet.

OSCAR. Why would anybody be interested in my feet? I have five toes, nothing special; nothing hard to figure out, right, I'm not complicated.

MANUELA. And I'm glad.

OSCAR. I know what I want. It's easy. Life is easy. You just have to make sure you win, that's all. Nothing else to it, dear. If I have a fever, I drink a shot of brandy; for headache a whiskey. An orphanage – that was the only thing I ever feared – but they didn't put me in one. I took care of myself. Here, do the cufflinks.

MANUELA. You're handsome, you know.

OSCAR. I'm never disappointed – I'll own the mansion up the street one day. That's what I want; that's what I'll get. I get everything I want.

MANUELA. You have me.

OSCAR. I don't worry. Ernesto is always worried, his nerves, his blood pressure, his toe hurts, Jesus, that's why Adelita goes looking...

MANUELA. My brother's delicate…

OSCAR. He's a coward. An affair, that's what he needs, with someone who'll slap him around a couple of times.

MANUELA. Don't be cruel.

OSCAR. That would reveal something to him. He'd know he was a coward and maybe start looking for his balls.

MANUELA. Stop talking about my brother that way.

OSCAR. Get me a glass of water. My mouth is dry from all this talking. Go and get it. Go, go, go.

(He hands her the glass. He gives her little kisses. She smiles and goes to the dining room. **ARTURO** *is sitting in the dining room drinking brandy.* **MANUELA** *pours a glass of water.)*

ARTURO. I once knew a little girl who sang to only me.

MANUELA. That was a long time ago, Papa. *(She blows him a kiss, walks to her room)*

ARTURO. I can still walk on water *(He drinks more brandy)*

*(**MANUELA** enters the bedroom.)*

MANUELA. Here, dear.

*(**OSCAR** drinks the water.)*

OSCAR. Manuela, sit, listen, I'll have to decide soon if your brother is worth his share. I keep him because he is your brother. I feel obligated, because I love you, I'm in the family now. What a family. Quite a family, bunch of infants, your brothers.

MANUELA. You don't think I'm a coward?

OSCAR. No.

MANUELA. I love you.

OSCAR. Time to go.

MANUELA. No. A few more minutes. Until I fall back asleep.

(She goes back to bed, **OSCAR** *watches her.* **MIGUEL** *enters the living room.)*

MIGUEL. Papa, time for work.

*(***ARTURO*** exits,* **ERNESTO** *enters the living room from the kitchen.)*

ERNESTO. Miguel, you added up the money wrong again last night.

MIGUEL. I was short. That's impossible.

ERNESTO. You were over.

MIGUEL. What a pleasant surprise.

ERNESTO. You don't pay attention when you're adding. You're not careful.

MIGUEL. I was in a hurry.

ERNESTO. You're always in a hurry. Be careful. If not, we'll have to do it together. I won't be able to trust you.

MIGUEL. You're going to teach me?

ERNESTO. If I have to.

*(***ADELITA*** starts to sing.)*

MIGUEL. I'll wait for the lesson.

ERNESTO. Don't be angry.

MIGUEL. I'm not.

*(***MIGUEL*** enters the porch,* **ERNESTO** *exits to the kitchen.)*

Good evening.

ADELITA. Daydreaming again.

MIGUEL. Wonderful dreams.

ADELITA. Hmmm, me too.

MIGUEL. I dreamed about the airplane.

ADELITA. That you invented it, or that you flew in it?

MIGUEL. Please. *(He grabs* **ADELITA***'s hand)*

ADELITA. Your brother is in the kitchen eating cake.

MIGUEL. Don't mention him.

ADELITA. You are not good.

MIGUEL. I'm not like Ernesto. Lunch tomorrow, at your house?

ADELITA. No. *(She hits him with her fan)* Tomorrow? I'll let you know. No. I'm sorry, I can't.

> *(***MIGUEL*** *exits to the street.* ***ADELITA*** *enters the living room.* ***MARIA JOSEFA*** *and* ***ERNESTO*** *enter from the kitchen.* ***ERNESTO*** *is eating cake.* ***MARIA JOSEFA*** *holds a cup of cafe with milk for him.)*

ERNESTO. Oscar's business ideas sure are good; one bus then two and so on. He says, "More tourists, more public transportation." Anyway, then he's thinking of hotels.

MARIA JOSEFA. More cafe, with milk, dear?

ERNESTO. No, Mama, water. And Adelita will get it.

MARIA JOSEFA. It's all right, Adelita. I'll get the water.

ADELITA. Fine.

ERNESTO. No, not fine, my mother's worked hard enough. Now it's my wife's turn.

ADELITA. She wants to do it.

ERNESTO. Let's not argue in front of my mother, please do it.

ADELITA. All right, water.

MARIA JOSEFA. Do you want another piece of cake? Wait, Adelita.

ERNESTO. Just water.

MARIA JOSEFA. Why? You didn't like it? I didn't put enough sugar, or did I put too much vanilla? Or is it the syrup, too much rum?

ERNESTO. Mama, my stomach hurts.

MARIA JOSEFA. Oh, I see.

ADELITA. Then just water? *(She smiles)*

ERNESTO. Yes. Just water, nothing else.

> *(***ADELITA*** *goes to the kitchen.)*

MARIA JOSEFA. Have you been eating at home?

ERNESTO. Sure, where else?

MARIA JOSEFA. Don't eat there, please. You know about her family and witchcraft. She would prefer if you were drugged.

ERNESTO. I have to trust her.

MARIA JOSEFA. No, you don't and –

ERNESTO. Oscar's other idea is sandwich shops all along the main highway with gasoline pumps.

MARIA JOSEFA. You shouldn't protect her; adultery…

ERNESTO. Adultery. You even know, even my mother knows.

(**ADELITA** *enters. She hands him a glass.*)

ADELITA. Water.

MARIA JOSEFA. Without a plate. I'll bring a plate. *(She takes glass from* **ERNESTO***)*
My son gets served with a plate.

ADELITA. Yes, Maria, of course, Maria Josefa, your son.

(**MARIA JOSEFA** *exits.*)

ERNESTO. Respect my mother, at least my mother.

ADELITA. I'm a mother. Your son's mother.

ERNESTO. That's the only reason I haven't beaten you to a pulp…no one in this town would stop me, adulteress.

ADELITA. Adulteress, yes adultery. Your accusation, I know. I'm so bored with you.

(**MARIA JOSEFA** *enters.*)

MARIA JOSEFA. Water, son. *(She hands him a glass with plate)*

ERNESTO. Thank you, Mama. *(He drinks, hands glass and plate back to her)*

MARIA JOSEFA. I'll take care of you. You and my grandson will live here, with me.

ADELITA. My son lives with me, you can have your son. If Ernesto had any courage, he'd be the one in charge.

MARIA JOSEFA. Adelita, what do you know about business?

ADELITA. Your husband's business is widely known.

MARIA JOSEFA. God forgives it in men, never in women. It will be hell for you.

ADELITA. And you, do you forgive?

MARIA JOSEFA. I don't forgive.

ADELITA. You are immune. Lucky you in heaven with a harp. Stop looking at me.

ERNESTO. I am looking for the truth.

ADELITA. You know the truth.

ERNESTO. I'm trying to see if there's anything good.

ADELITA. You had your chance.

ERNESTO. Damn you!

ADELITA. Weakling.

MARIA JOSEFA. Stop it.

ADELITA. Oscar's slave!

ERNESTO. Not in front of my mother.

ADELITA. Be a man, weakling.

MARIA JOSEFA. Get out.

ADELITA. You know the truth.

ERNESTO. Liar, it's till death do you part, Adelita.

(**ADELITA** *goes to the porch.*)

I'm sorry, Mama. I'm sorry you had to see the fight. I'm sorry.

MARIA JOSEFA. I know, dear. I'm sorry, too.

(**ARTURO** *enters in work clothes.*)

ARTURO. Ernesto, come with me for a drink, before I go to work.

ERNESTO. No.

ARTURO. Ernesto, you should spend less time with your mother and more time making your wife happy.

ERNESTO. You have to prove yourself, don't you?

ARTURO. Prove myself, no.

ERNESTO. You have to think you're the best?

ARTURO. No.

ERNESTO. You have to prove yourself with every woman.

ARTURO. No. Maria, go in the kitchen, I want a piece of cake.

MARIA JOSEFA. You don't need to protect me.

ARTURO. Maria, please go.

(MARIA JOSEFA *lights a cigarette and begins to smoke it.*)

ERNESTO. Why don't I feel it, why doesn't my flesh feel it?

ARTURO. I don't know. Maybe I didn't do the right thing.

ERNESTO. What?

ARTURO. I should have bought you someone on your fifteenth birthday. I should have taken you to a whorehouse.

ERNESTO. You should have, she cuts off my balls. She takes my guts out. I'm everybody's fool. I don't want to think about it, but it's all I think about. That I'm betrayed, that I'm made fun of. I wanted all the good things. I wanted to be like Joseph was to Mary,

ARTURO. Leave her.

ERNESTO. I'd rather go to whores than go to her.

ARTURO. Then go to whores.

ERNESTO. I hope she dies.

ARTURO. Forget her. You need to be there with Oscar making all the decisions. I want you to represent us, to represent me. We own the bus company. Not just Oscar.

ERNESTO. Do you think witchcraft works?

ARTURO. Poison does.

ERNESTO. Hmmm. You'll be proud of me. Don't worry, Papa, I'll be in charge. I need another piece of cake.

MARIA JOSEFA. How big?

ERNESTO. No, Mama, you rest, I'll get it myself. (*He goes into the kitchen*)

MARIA JOSEFA. I'll be asleep, don't wake me; be quiet when you walk in. Don't put the sheets off me in the middle of the night.

ARTURO. Yes, fine. (*Pause*) And you leave Ernesto alone.

MARIA JOSEFA. He is mine, my son.

ARTURO. You feed him too much –

MARIA JOSEFA. He's pleasantly plump, he looks handsome that way. I have to take care of him. I have to be kind to him.

ARTURO. He has a wife!

MARIA JOSEFA. She's the image of you.

ARTURO. I am everything a husband is supposed to be. I provide. My business provided the money for this new enterprise. It is still my gamble. I am still the one in control. So stop stuffing my son with lies about me.

MARIA JOSEFA. I never turned him against you. You're his father. I tell all of them to love you. I know we all have weaknesses. I know what a wife, a mother is supposed to do…

ARTURO. Desire cannot be control. I am not expected to control that. And you –

MARIA JOSEFA. And I stop you? Do I? Arturo?!

ARTURO. You're a good woman.

MARIA JOSEFA. Decent?!

ARTURO. Yes, Maria Josefa. Decent.

(**ERNESTO** *enters eating cake.*)

How many pieces today?

ERNESTO. This is the third piece, I think. Oh sweets, Mama makes the best cake, better than any bakery.

ARTURO. Think about what I told you.

ERNESTO. Yes, I will.

ARTURO. Time to get to work.

(**ARTURO** *kisses* **MARIA JOSEFA** *lightly on the forehead.*)

MARIA JOSEFA. Till tomorrow. In the morning I won't wake you.

ARTURO. Fine, Maria.

(**ARTURO** *goes to the porch,* **ADELITA** *looks at him.*)

ERNESTO. I'll bring you cafe later.

MARIA JOSEFA. Do you love him?

ERNESTO. Yes, Mama, I love both of you, you gave me everything.

(**ARTURO** *and* **ADELITA** *are on the porch.*)

ARTURO. Adelita, you're a marvel, you get lovelier every year, instead of older.

ADELITA. Maybe I'll divorce him.

ARTURO. I'll divorce Maria if you do.

ADELITA. And we'll live happily ever after?

ARTURO. For a few minutes at least.

ADELITA. They'll burn us at the stake.

ARTURO. We'll keep it to ourselves, don't let anyone know anything you do in this town.

ADELITA. Yes.

ARTURO. You would be worth it.

ADELITA. Thank you.

(*Blackout. Lights up on* **MARIO** *and* **OSCAR** *entering the living room.*)

OSCAR. What can I do?

MARIO. Do what you have to do, you have to do it, do it.

OSCAR. Would you?

MARIO. For the good of the business?

OSCAR. Yes.

MARIO. I'd do anything for the good of the business.

OSCAR. I'm going to give Ernesto another chance.

MARIO. Another chance.

OSCAR. One, one more chance.

MARIO. And if it's hopeless?

OSCAR. You'll be second in command.

MARIO. Thank you.

OSCAR. Ernesto will feel defeated.

MARIO. I'll reconcile with my brother.

OSCAR. Will you be able to take care of that?

MARIO. Are you kidding, I'm the one who sweats in ice and is cool in the middle of a fire.

(**ADELITA** *sings "Tea for Two."*)

OSCAR. Tell him another week.

MARIO. I will, have a good time.

OSCAR. I will.

(**OSCAR** *exits to the street.* **MARIO** *crosses to the porch.*)

MARIO. Ernesto.

ERNESTO. Mario.

MARIO. I'm out on the porch.

ERNESTO. A minute.

(**ADELITA** *is singing.*)

MARIO. The singing parrot.

ADELITA. Who?

MARIO. You. You are the singing parrot.

ADELITA. I have a good voice. *(Sings)* "Nobody near us to see us or hear us. No friends or relations on weekend vacations." It's nice to listen to. Sounds respectable.

MARIO. Respectable?!

ADELITA. I have a respectable voice. It doesn't crack.

MARIO. That's true, it doesn't crack, but it's not great. People wouldn't pay to hear it.

ADELITA. I'm not asking anyone to pay.

MARIO. Then why do it, Adelita?

ADELITA. To entertain myself, Mario. To amuse myself, to hear myself.

(**ERNESTO** *enters.*)

MARIO. Ernesto, Oscar asked my advice. I stood by you, you know that.

ERNESTO. Thank you.

MARIO. Oscar told me to tell you, you have one more week.

ERNESTO. A week? What do I do wrong? I work hard. Why are you all so concerned?

MARIO. You're not pushy. You're not aggressive.

ERNESTO. I do my job.

MARIO. Oscar has to do all the bargaining, make all the deals so we have good routes. If you are second in command you have to wheel and deal, get other people to trust you. To believe in you. You have to have the kind of reputation people can believe in.

ERNESTO. Only Oscar can do that.

MARIO. No…

ADELITA. Can you wheel and deal?

MARIO. Absolutely. Yes I can.

ADELITA. Lucky you.

(**MIGUEL** *enters.*)

MIGUEL. Papa got shot! Papa was shot!

ERNESTO. Shot! Shot! Shot!

ADELITA. Why? WHY?

MARIO. He was at the bus yard?

MIGUEL. Oscar's with him now. He wants you, Mario.

ADELITA. Arturo, Arturo? Arturo?...Ernesto.

MIGUEL. Ernesto, he's dying.

ERNESTO. My father is dying. My father?

(**MARIA JOSEFA** *stands in the front door and listens to them talk.*)

ADELITA. Who shot him?

MIGUEL. It must have been Beatrice's husband. Papa was walking down the street, Beatrice's husband must have followed him down the block, it happened in front of the bus yard. He must have heard about Beatrice and Papa. He shot Papa in the back.

MARIO. Beatrice the American?

MARIA JOSEFA. Beatrice, the adulteress. Beatrice the cheat. Beatrice, the fraud. He got shot because of her. Don't forget. He who was never going to bring it home. Who kept it discreet. Where's Manuela?

MARIO. In her room.

MARIA JOSEFA. Good, I don't want her to know about that American.

MARIO. You're right, Mama. She's his daughter, she must be protected.

MARIA JOSEFA. Is he going to be all right?

MARIO. Yes, Mama. He'll be fine.

MARIA JOSEFA. I'll stay here with Manuela.

MIGUEL. Oscar wants Mario to go.

MARIA JOSEFA. Did anyone see it happen?

MIGUEL. No, Oscar found him on the ground.

MARIA JOSEFA. Good. We'll keep it our secret.

MARIO. Of course.

*(***MARIA JOSEFA*** and ***ERNESTO*** enter the living room.)*

MARIA JOSEFA. I spend my life with him looking at me. He made me feel wanted once. Ernesto, you go too, come back and get me when the doctors are through with him. You should be with him. Go be a good son.

*(***ERNESTO*** starts to walk out. ***ADELITA*** follows him.)*

ERNESTO. You stay here and pray.

*(Blackout. Lights up. ***MARIA JOSEFA*** kneeling with her rosary. Long pause.)*

MARIA JOSEFA. I can't remember one prayer.

*(***MANUELA*** enters.)*

MANUELA. Where is everyone?

MARIA JOSEFA. Your father had a little accident. Don't worry, he'll be fine.

MANUELA. What kind of accident?

MARIA JOSEFA. He was shot in the arm.

MANUELA. Shot?

MARIA JOSEFA. Help me remember the prayer.

MANUELA. In the name of the Father and of the Son…

MARIA JOSEFA. Now I remember.

MANUELA. Oh.

MARIA JOSEFA. What's wrong?

MANUELA. The baby kicked.

MARIA JOSEFA. He's telling us to pray.

MANUELA. She does it all the time.

MARIA JOSEFA. That means he's strong.

(ADELITA *enters.*)

ADELITA. Here are the candles. I'll light them.

MARIA JOSEFA. Learn from his mistakes. Learn from it, Adelita.

MANUELA. Did they rob him?

MARIA JOSEFA. Let's pray.

MANUELA. Where were we?

MARIA JOSEFA. Another Hail Mary.

MARIA JOSEFA, MANUELA, ADELITA. Hail Mary full of grace, the Lord is with thee. Blessed art thou among women and blessed is the fruit of thy womb, Jesus. Holy Mary mother of God, pray for us sinners now and at the hour of our death, amen.

MANUELA. We should go and be with him.

ADELITA. I think so. Let's go.

MARIA JOSEFA. No. They'll probably bring him home in a little while.

MANUELA. Are you sure he's not hurt?

MARIA JOSEFA. It's nothing serious, pray.

ADELITA. I don't know, Maria.

MARIA JOSEFA. Adelita, he was shot in the arm, a surface wound, that's all.

MANUELA. Maybe they lied to you?

MARIA JOSEFA. Of course not.

MANUELA. Everything scares me. He'll be safe?

MARIA JOSEFA. Yes, I'm sure.

MANUELA. You promise me?

MARIA JOSEFA. I promise, dear. It's just a small wound, nothing to worry about.

ADELITA. Not in the arm, Maria –

MARIA JOSEFA. In the arm, Adelita! Remember. Is the baby calmer?

MANUELA. No.

ADELITA. Oh.

MARIA JOSEFA. Still moving around?

MANUELA. Yes.

ADELITA. They do that a lot.

MANUELA. Not as much as today.

MARIA JOSEFA. He's getting ready.

MANUELA. Maybe she will come today, maybe today will be her birthday.

MARIA JOSEFA. Pray, girls, time to pray.

(All three pray silently and quickly; mechanically they do three Hail Mary's. **ERNESTO** *and* **MIGUEL** *enter.)*

MIGUEL. Mama, he's asking for you. We came to get you.

MARIA JOSEFA. How is he?

MIGUEL. Fine, Mama, fine.

MARIA JOSEFA. For once he'll have to listen. He'll hate it. He hates to be told what to do. Basques are like that. That's why the Spaniards kicked them out. The Spaniards told them what they were supposed to do, but they were always rebelling. They called themselves something peculiar… *(She thinks)* "Anarchists." So the Spanish threw them out. He has books about it in our bedroom. We should burn them. We shouldn't have books like that around us. I don't think he even believed in Baby Jesus. He was wild man.

MIGUEL. He has balls.

MARIA JOSEFA. Build businesses. Now it's up to the two of you.

ERNESTO. You're right, Mama.

MARIA JOSEFA. It's time to face him. Manuela, you stay here.

MANUELA. Why?

MARIA JOSEFA. He is in a hospital. You don't want to catch a disease. Continue the rosary while you wait.

MANUELA. Tell him I love him. Adelita, will you stay with me?

ADELITA. Yes.

(*The rest exit.* MANUELA *kneels and then* ADELITA *kneels.*)

What prayer were we up to?

MANUELA. The fifth Hail Mary.

ADELITA. Thirty-five more to go.

MANUELA. Maybe we were up to the middle of Our Father. I never know what I'm up to when I do the rosary. Maybe the seventh Hail Mary? Maybe we should start from the beginning. I think it's a sin if you pick it up in the middle. Do you remember the rules, Adelita?

ADELITA. No, I forget. We better make sure we're doing it the right way.

MANUELA. Let's begin at the beginning. In the name of the Father and the Son.... Oh. She's been kicking all afternoon. Isn't it odd, a baby is such a saintly thing, and the act of making him or her makes one feel so wicked.

ADELITA. You feel wicked?

MANUELA. Yes, I'm not Papa's good girl anymore. (*She cries*)

ADELITA. Your father is a hypocrite.

MANUELA. Don't speak about Papa that way. My father is strict, proper and moral.

ADELITA. To impress you.

MANUELA. You want to put everyone in the soup you're in.

ADELITA. I flirt. That's all.

MANUELA. Please stop your lies.

ADELITA. They are lying to you. Your father was with Beatrice. The American. Her husband...shot Arturo in the back because of adultery. Because of sex.

MANUELA. You are lying. I do not believe you.

ADELITA. Even your mother knows.

MANUELA. I'll pull your hair and kick your teeth in, slut.

(ADELITA *slaps* MANUELA. MANUELA *slaps her back.*)

ADELITA. It's not fair, you're pregnant. I can't hurt you. Let's stop.

MANUELA. All right. I'll stop for the baby, I'll stop. *(She kneels)* In the name of the...

ADELITA. Manuela...

MANUELA. Let me pray.

ADELITA. Why am I not allowed to talk in this house? Why don't you consider me a part of the life here in this family? I get tolerated, that's all...

MANUELA. Hail Mary full of –

ADELITA. I've been the burden you all struggle with, your family's embarrassment.

MANUELA. Please stop, I don't want to hear anymore.

ADELITA. Beatrice's husband found your father, he searched for your father. He shot and the shot succeeded. They're lying to you to keep you in line. Your father is dying.

MANUELA. Get out, Adelita.

ADELITA. If Ernesto wants me, I'm at my mother's, with his baby. *(She exits to the porch)*

MANUELA. My father is dying. *(She cries. She reads from a prayer book)*

(OSCAR *walks onto the back porch, sees* ADELITA.)

"The Lord created man out of earth and turns him back to it again. He gave men a few days, a limited time."

ADELITA. I told her about Beatrice and Arturo, She knows...

OSCAR. Tell me why, Adelita? Tell me.

MANUELA. "He made him tongue and eyes and a mind for thinking."

ADELITA. She should know that the men in this town are

cheats and liars and a bunch of hypocrites…

OSCAR. I could say that about a few of the women…

ADELITA. No. The women in this town pretend, they pretend to each other that nothing is going on..

MANUELA. "He filled him with knowledge and understanding, and showed him good and evil…" *(She touches her stomach)*

ADELITA. … then we accuse each other. But with you men we are taught to look the other way and forgive and smile. *(She smiles at **OSCAR**)*

OSCAR. You are a whore.

MANUELA. "…and showed him the majesty of his work…"

ADELITA. I am a saint compared to you men. You know that. You know what everybody is doing.

(**ADELITA** *exits.* **OSCAR** *enters the living room.* **MANUELA** *cries in his arms.)*

OSCAR. My darling, sweetie, my china doll. I'll take care of you, my piece of caramel.

MANUELA. You do love me?

OSCAR. Yes. On my mother's grave.

MANUELA. And the first time you look at a woman and you want her, tell me so I'm not blind.

OSCAR. That'll never happen.

MANUELA. But if it happens, you'll tell me, promise me. I'm not a coward. I have to be the only one in your thoughts every second, and if it ever stops, I want to know.

OSCAR. You are always in my thoughts. Every time I look at a passenger getting in the bus, I think, another dime for Manuela and what she has inside.

MANUELA. If you ever touch someone else – I could never let go if it wasn't you – oh, it kicked again. *(She laughs)*

OSCAR. Can I put my hand and feel it? *(He does)* What should we name him?

MANUELA. After my father, Arturo. *(She cries)* I love my father.

OSCAR. And if it's a girl, Manuela.

MANUELA. No, I hate my name.

OSCAR. Carmen.

MANUELA. No, this horrible woman I knew was named Carmen. I could never call my baby that.

OSCAR. Tamara.

MANUELA. That sounds like a tango dancer.

OSCAR. Dun, dun dun dun, tra la la la la.

(They start to tango.)

And she'll be able to tango and waltz.

MANUELA. How refined. *(She laughs)*

OSCAR. And never worry, because what's inside you, the baby Tamara, Arturo, Carmen –

MANUELA. Sonia?

OSCAR. Sonia, yes, Sonia is going to look like a millionaire.

MANUELA. And you'll want me? Till we're dust?

OSCAR. Someday, I'll buy cars and boats and go on vacations to Spain for you.

MANUELA. If it ever changes tell me. You're the only person I respect.

OSCAR. I will work only for you, struggle for you and cheat people for you. You, my family.

MANUELA. Yes, our family, you and me and what's inside of me.

OSCAR. We'll put your brothers on salary, not shares but regular salaries.

MANUELA. If you think it's best.

OSCAR. It's a unique concept, but it assures perfect results.

MANUELA. If you think it's right...

OSCAR. In business you must blend meticulously all the ingredients. Number one, the boss equals the owners; number two, then there are the workers; if you have these two things clearly defined, it'll work one hundred percent of the time. In any type of business…It's the way they blend cafe…

MANUELA. Kahwah. *(She laughs)*

OSCAR. The right beans together make black gold, for white gods.

(**MARIA JOSEFA** *and Mario enter.*)

MARIO. Oscar, you're safe, you're here.

MARIA JOSEFA. Manuela, I have to talk to Oscar. I need a few moments with Oscar.

MANUELA. Mama, I want to know everything that goes on!

OSCAR. Yes, Maria Josefa?

MARIO. He's dead. Papa is dead!

(**MARIO** *starts to cry.* **OSCAR** *helps* **MANUELA** *onto a chair, she is also crying.*)

OSCAR. Have they found Beatrice's husband?!

MARIA JOSEFA. It was not Beatrice's husband.

MANUELA. Stop lying, I know.

MARIA JOSEFA. What do you know?

MANUELA. Adelita told me the truth.

MARIA JOSEFA. It was the capital warning us. It was a threat. One of President Machado's men came up to me. He stood next to me while they were taking your father's body away. And whispered: "This is only the beginning, tell your group to get wise."

OSCAR. But…. They've been taken care of. The cooperative took care of that!

MARIO. But they want it all, they want the rest of us to be slaves… just like Papa said.

MARIA JOSEFA. We won't let them, you and I cannot let them, Oscar. We have to advance.

OSCAR. Of course, that's what Arturo wanted. Mario, when we are in control we'll slit their throats, one after the other, like at a chicken farm.

MARIO. Is that what Father wanted?

MANUELA. Yes!

MARIO. Here's the money.

OSCAR. Good.

MARIO. No one stole anything. Are they going to kill us all!

OSCAR. I will not live in poverty. I will not be a pauper; and my children will only see wealth…. we'll pretend they didn't say it.

MARIA JOSEFA. Yes!

OSCAR. Maria Josefa, her husband killed him, domestic.

MARIA JOSEFA. That's right.

OSCAR. But we'll be on the lookout. On our guard.

MARIO. No, there has to be some kind of justice.

OSCAR. The only justice is money.

MARIO. They have to pay.

OSCAR. Who killed your husband, Maria Josefa?

MARIA JOSEFA. A jealous husband.

MANUELA. That's right, Mario. It was Beatrice's husband, it wasn't politics. He probably sent that other man there to start a rumor to cover up his act. It was Beatrice that killed Papa.

MARIA JOSEFA. Mario, your father was killed by?

MARIO. No, please Mama.

OSCAR. Your father was killed by a…

(Pause.)

MARIO. By a woman's lust and betrayal.

OSCAR. Give me the money. I'll count the money, you mourn.

*(**MARIO** hands **MANUELA** the money.)*

MARIA JOSEFA. Yes. Go be with your father. Dress him in his white suit.

*(**MARIO** exits.)*

OSCAR. You ladies go dress in black, I'll take care of business.

MARIA JOSEFA. No, Manuela will count the money, she's the best at mathematics. Manuela will count the money from now on.

MANUELA. Why?

MARIA JOSEFA. You represent both of us, both our interests.

(OSCAR *hands* MANUELA *the money.*)

OSCAR. China doll, count.

(*He touches her and then exits.* MANUELA *starts to count the money.*)

MARIA JOSEFA. Do a good job, suppress your feelings and work. Be in control. That's why we cut our hair.

MANUELA. We will be happy, Oscar and me.

MARIA JOSEFA. That will be my prayer, that you're the lucky one, the one that doesn't have to keep it all inside, all a secret.

MANUELA. This is for her, Mama. She'll be able to afford to be arrogant.

MARIA JOSEFA. She won't be dishonored like me.

MANUELA. Oscar will buy it all for her.

MARIA JOSEFA. No. We will buy it all for her.

MANUELA. Feel, Mama, she's kicking hard. She'll make you happy. Sonia, Sonia Luz Hernandez,=.

MARIA JOSEFA. Ripoll.

MANUELA. I have to ask Oscar where to hide the money.

(*She starts to exit*)

MARIA JOSEFA. Let me know where he hides it.

MANUELA. Yes.

(MANUELA *exits.* MARIA JOSEFA *lights a cigarette.*)

MARIA JOSEFA. Arturo the Basque and Maria Josefa… (*She smokes*) Arturo, who won? Maria Josefa. Because, Maria Josefa is alive. (*She smokes*)

(*Blackout.*)

END OF PLAY